when I'm BIG

ISBN 0-439-24452-8

12 11 10 9 8 7 6 5 4 3 2 1   1 2 3 4 5 6/0

Printed in the U.S.A.   08

First Scholastic printing, January 2001

Book design by Nila Aye

The text of this book is set in Avante Garde Bold.
The illustrations are designed on an Apple Macintosh computer
using Adobe Illustrator software.

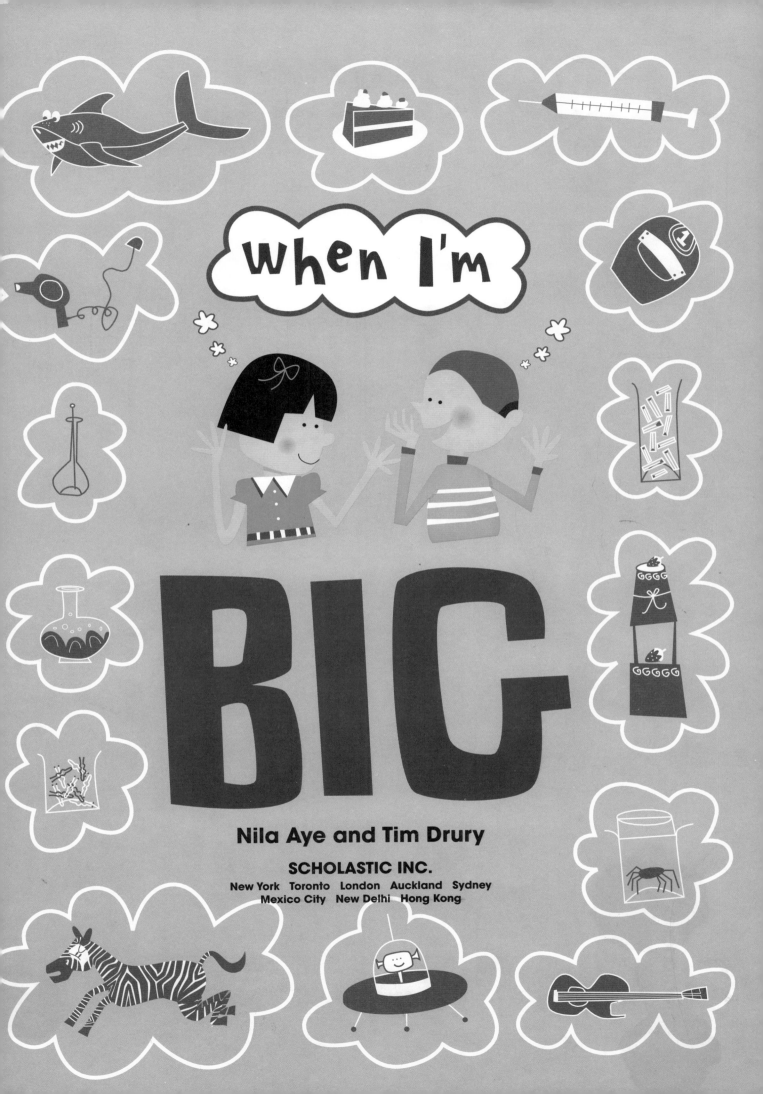

when I'm

BIG

Nila Aye and Tim Drury

SCHOLASTIC INC.

New York Toronto London Auckland Sydney
Mexico City New Delhi Hong Kong

Mo and Joe watched the rain, waiting for the sun.

They couldn't play outside today, which wasn't very fun.

"When we are big," said Mo to Joe, "we won't be bored again.

We'll always do exciting things, even in the rain!"

"I might be a **scientist**—that would be good!
I'd stay in my lab all day long if I could.
Perhaps I could cure lots of nasty diseases—
my special potion would stop coughs and sneezes!"

"My turn," said Joe, "and I love the sea,
so I'll be a **diver!** It's the best job for me.
I'll watch out for sharks as I swim very deep
in search of a shipwreck and treasure to keep!"

"Hairdressing!" said Mo. "That's what I'll do.
I'll need scissors and combs and lots of shampoo.
Then I'll create some fantastic new styles.
The line to my shop will stretch on for miles."

"I'd be a **race-car driver** with a big, fast car.

What a life that would be—the best job by far!

I would need skill and nerve to stay in the lead,

and I'd roar past the flag at breathtaking speed!"

"The world is so big, I would love to **explore**

all the deserts and mountains and jungles and more.

My travels would take me so far, far away,

it might take me years, but I'd come home one day."

"If I were a **chef** and I knew how to bake,

I could open a restaurant and choose what to make.

There'd be roast chicken dinners and pizzas and pies.

For dessert there'd be fudge cakes—all giant size!"

candy

chocolate drops

powder

potatoes

"I've got an idea — I'll be a **vet**.

There's nothing as sad as a sick little pet!

I'd see many creatures, some great and some small.

But I'd have to work hard to cure them all."

"I could be a **pop star** and have lots of fun.
Then I'd make records and be number one!
People would whistle my songs in the street
or see me on TV and dance to the beat!"

recording

PRODUCER

"I'll join the circus to learn the **trapeze**
and practice until I can swing up with ease.
I'll do my most dangerous tricks for the crowd,
so that, when I finish, they'll clap very loud!"

"I'll be a **spaceman,** with a space suit and rocket.
(I should keep a laser gun safe in my pocket.)
I'll find a new planet that no one has spotted
and leave a flag there to show that I've got it."

The game stopped when Mother called, "It's time to eat.

Have you tidied your room yet? I do hope it's neat."

"But Mom," answered Joe, "how can you think of our room?

Mo's joined the circus, and I'm going to the moon!"